Counting Crocodiles

Counting Crocodiles

by JUDY SIERRA

Illustrated by WILL HILLENBRAND

Voyager Books
Harcourt, Inc.

Orlando   Austin   New York   San Diego   Toronto   London

For information about permission to reproduce selections
from this book, write to trade.permissions@hmhco.com or to
Permissions, Houghton Mifflin Harcourt Publishing Com-
pany, 3 Park Avenue, 19th Floor, New York, New York 10016.

www.hmhco.com

Voyager Books is a trademark of Harcourt, Inc., registered
in the United States of America and/or other jurisdictions.

The Library of Congress has cataloged the hardcover
edition as follows:
Sierra, Judy.
Counting crocodiles/written by Judy Sierra;
illustrated by Will Hillenbrand.
p.   cm.
Summary: By using her ability to count, a clever monkey
outwits the hungry crocodiles that stand between her and
a banana tree on another island across the sea.
[1. Monkeys—Fiction. 2. Crocodiles—Fiction.
3. Counting. 4. Stories in rhyme.]
I. Hillenbrand, Will, ill. II. Title.
PZ8.3.S577Co   1997
[E]—dc20   95-48787
ISBN 978-0-15-200192-6
ISBN 978-0-15-216356-3 pb

SCP   25 24 23 22 21 20 19
4500607003

The illustrations in this book were done in oil, oil pastel,
watercolor, and gouache on vellum.
The display type was set in Oz Poster Condensed.
The text type was set in Stone Informal.
Color separations by United Graphic Pte. Ltd., Singapore
Printed and bound by RR Donnelley, China
Production supervision by Sandra Grebenar and Wendi Taylor
Designed by Kaelin Chappell and Will Hillenbrand

*Note: This story is based on a Pan-Asian folktale in
which a trickster animal (a monkey, a rabbit, or a
mouse deer) persuades crocodiles or sharks to form a
bridge over water, under the pretext of counting them.*

For Will Hillenbrand
—J. S.

For Judy Sierra and my son, Ian
—W. H.

On an island in the middle of the Sillabobble Sea

lived a clever little monkey in a sour lemon tree.

She ate lemons boiled and fried,

steamed, sautéed, pureed, and dried.

She ate lemons till she cried,

"I'm all puckered up inside!"

Then across that sea so wide,

a banana tree she spied.

"How delectable," she sighed.

"I would love to take a trip across the Sillabobble Sea

and carry back a stack of sweet bananas from that tree."

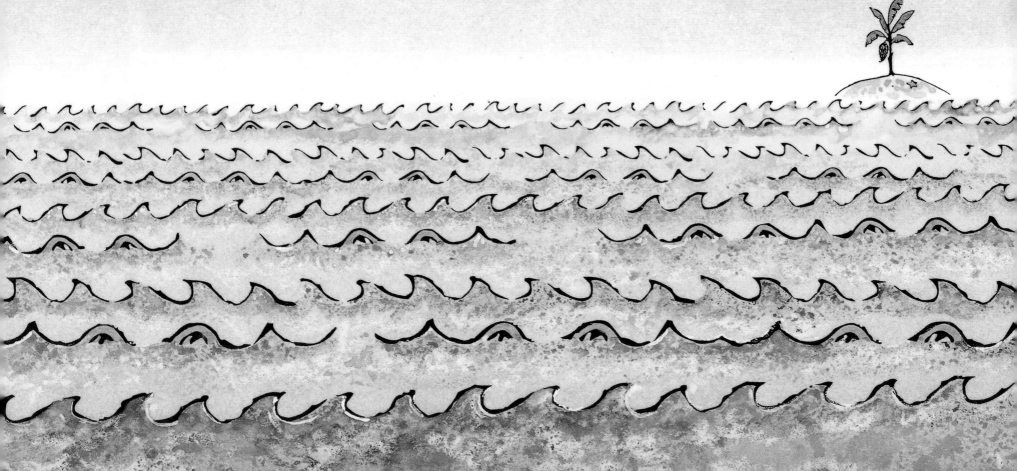

The Sillabobble crocodiles thought they were truly cool,

and they looked upon those waters as their private swimming pool.

They appeared to be quite vicious,

feasting fearlessly on fishes.

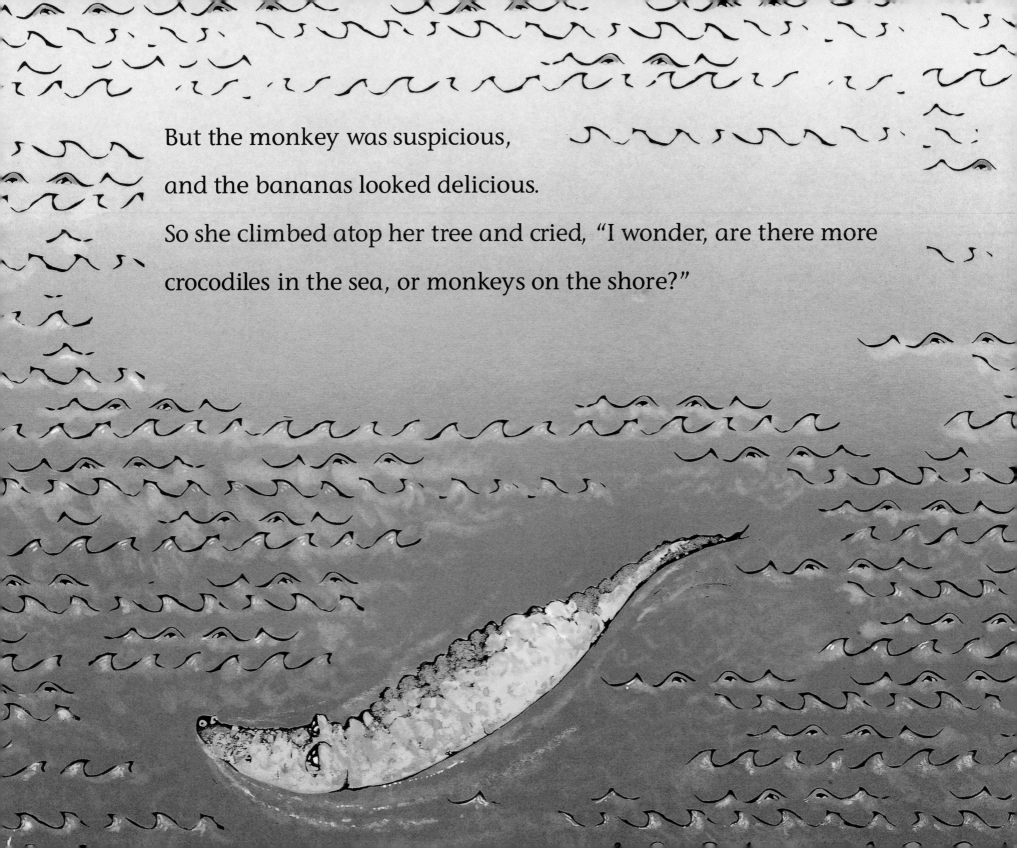

But the monkey was suspicious,

and the bananas looked delicious.

So she climbed atop her tree and cried, "I wonder, are there more

crocodiles in the sea, or monkeys on the shore?"

One crusty croc who chanced to hear her

snorted. "It could not be clearer

that lurking just below the waves are crocodiles galore.

Why, head to tail, we'd reach across the sea!" the reptile roared.

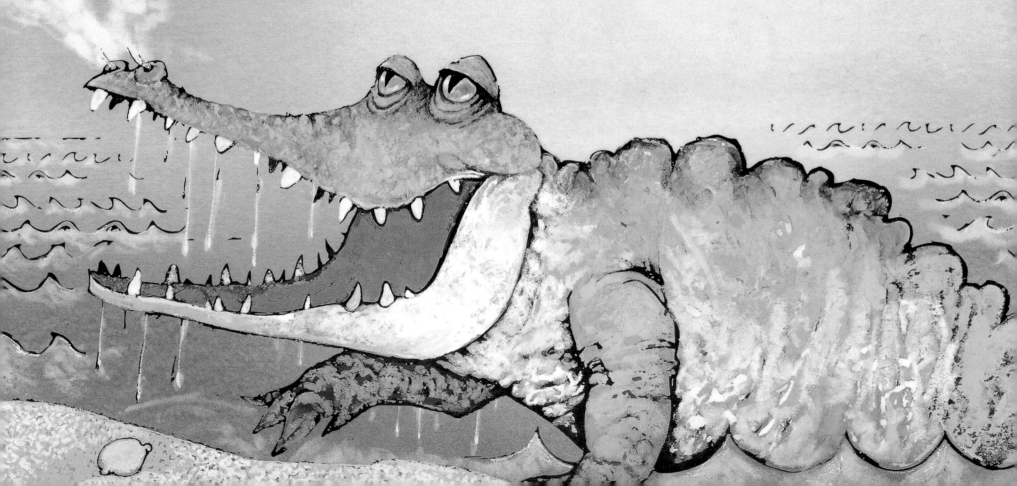

With those words he disappeared into the dark and salty sea, and brought back his entire crocodilian family.

"Just look at us! I have a hunch

you've never seen a bigger bunch.

(Later be our guest for lunch.)

We're all lined up and waiting, Monkey. Will you count us, please?"

She counted one crocodile with a great big smile,

Two crocs resting on rocks,

Three crocs rocking in a box,

Four crocs building with blocks,

Five crocs tickling a fox,

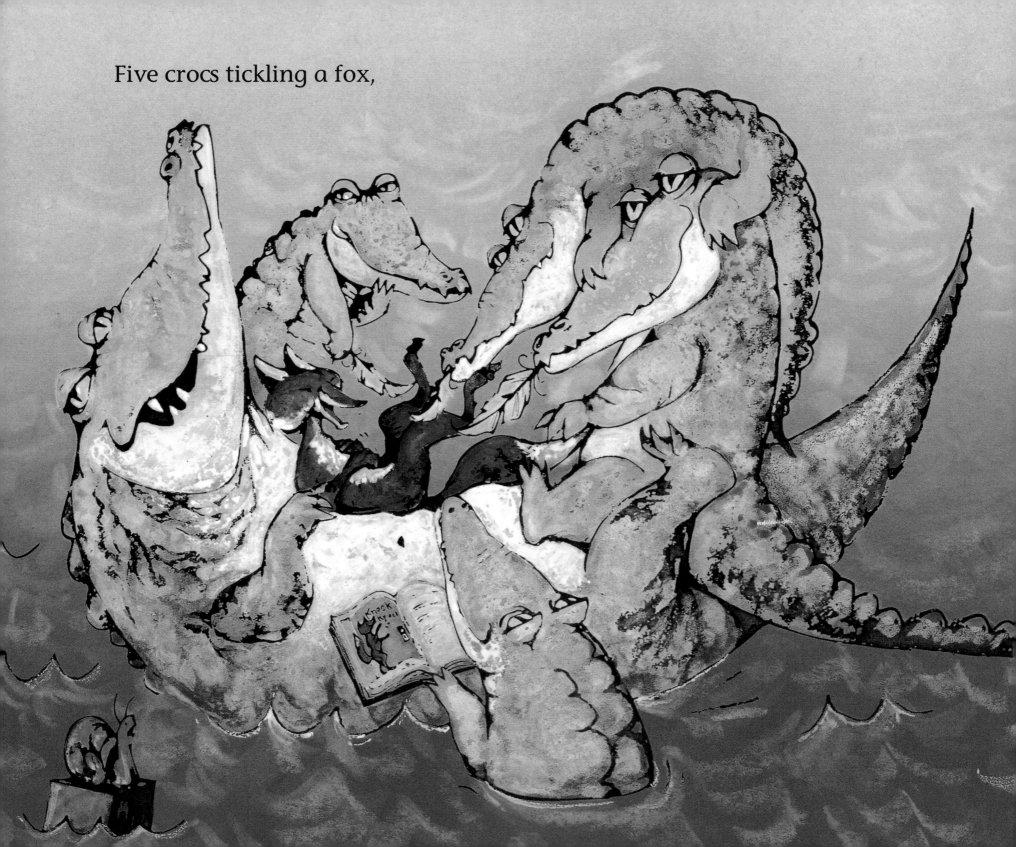

Six crocs with pink Mohawks,

Seven crocs juggling clocks,

Eight crocs in polka-dot socks,

Nine crocs with chicken pox,

And ten crocs dressed like Goldilocks.

The crocodiles were dancing and cavorting in the slime.

Impatiently they asked, "How many of us did you find?"

With her mouth full of bananas,

the monkey scolded, "Mind your manners!

Line up now, crocodiles!

I need to count you *one more time*."

She counted ten crocs dressed like Goldilocks,

Nine crocs with chicken pox,

Eight crocs in polka-dot socks,

Seven crocs juggling clocks,

Six crocs with pink Mohawks,

Five crocs tickling a fox,

Four crocs building with blocks,

Three crocs rocking in a box,

Two crocs resting on rocks,

And one crocodile with a great big smile.

As the monkey jumped ashore and scurried up her lemon tree,

the crocodiles below cried out, "How many, then, *are* we?

Tell us NOW!" The crocs all howled.

"Just enough ..." The monkey scowled.

"Just enough to make a bridge across the Sillabobble Sea, but not enough to catch a clever monkey like me!"